To The
Boys
+ Girls of
ST. PAUL'S
School

BLURT, BLURT!
STOP BLURTING!

Robert Krauz
1982

Mert
the Blurt

by Robert Kraus

pictures by Jose Aruego & Ariane Dewey

Windmill Books/Simon & Schuster
New York

Text copyright © 1980 by Robert Kraus
Illustrations copyright © 1980 by Jose Aruego and Ariane Dewey

Published by Windmill Books, Inc., and
Simon & Schuster, a Division of Gulf & Western Corporation
Simon & Schuster Building
1230 Avenue of the Americas
New York, New York 10020

WINDMILL BOOKS and colophon are trademarks of Windmill Books, Inc.,
registered in the U.S. Patent and Trademark Office.

Manufactured in the United States of America

10 9 8 7 6 5 4 3 2 1

Library of Congress Cataloging in Publication Data

Kraus, Robert
  Mert the blurt.

  SUMMARY: A blabbermouth, with whom no secret is
safe, finds a special niche in the news world.
  [1. Frogs—Fiction] I. Aruego, Jose. II. Dewey,
Ariane. III. Title.
PZ7.K868Me   [E]   80-14508
ISBN 0-671-96265-5

7646

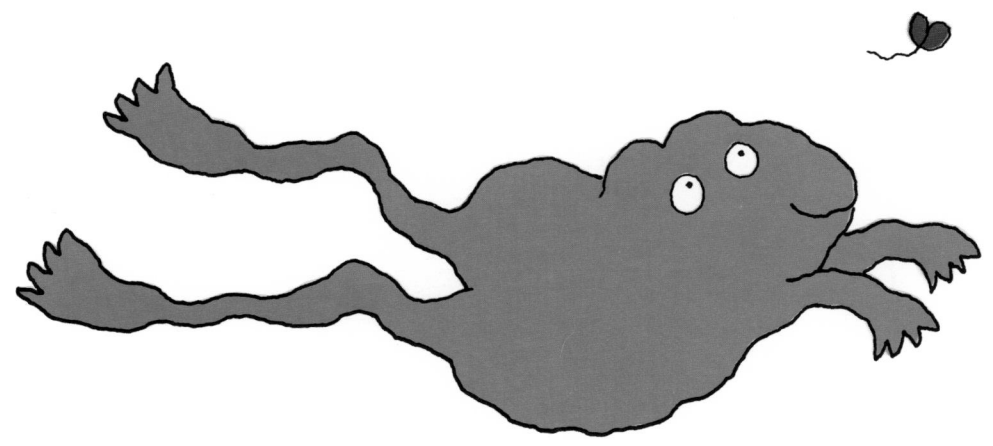

Mert was a blurt.

"Blurt, blurt, blurt," went Mert, Mert, Mert.

"Hold your tongue, Mert," said Mert's father.

Mert held his tongue but Mert still went, "Blurt, blurt, blurt."

Mert blurted out all the family secrets to everyone he met.

"My father wears long johns when he roller-skates!"

"My mother wears a bikini when she discos!"

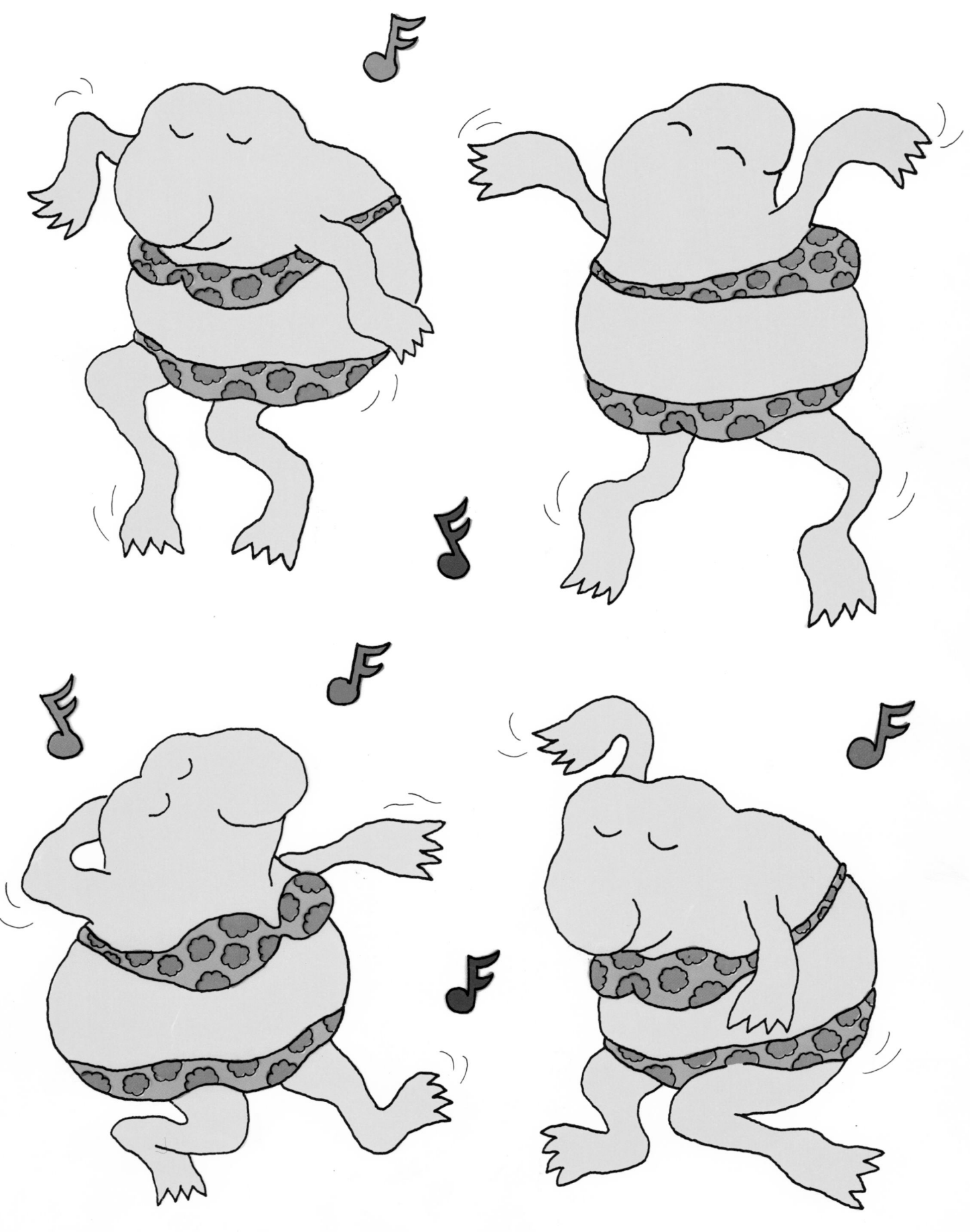

"Is nothing sacred?" cried Mert's father.

"Not to me, Pop," blurted Mert.

**"Aunt Patti wears
soft contact lenses."**

**"Uncle Max
wears disguises."**

"Uncle Benny drives a gas guzzler."

"Aunt Martha goes
skinny-dipping.

Uncle Bernie
likes frogs' legs

and I saw Mommy kissing Santa Claus."

The Creeps next door were shocked.

The Nincompoops in the rear were appalled.

All the relatives on both sides of the family were mortified.
They never told Mert anything for fear he would blurt it out.

But Mert found things out anyway.
And went, "Blurt! Blurt! Blurt!"

"Why does Mert blurt?" cried Mert's mother.

"Who knows, who cares?" cried Mert's father.
All the world hates a blurter.

BLURT!

BLURT!

BLURT!

BLURT!

BLURT!

BLURT!

BLURT!

BLURT!

"Oh what will become of Mert?" cried Mert's mother and father.

What became of Mert was...

...he became a famous T.V. news anchorman and now:

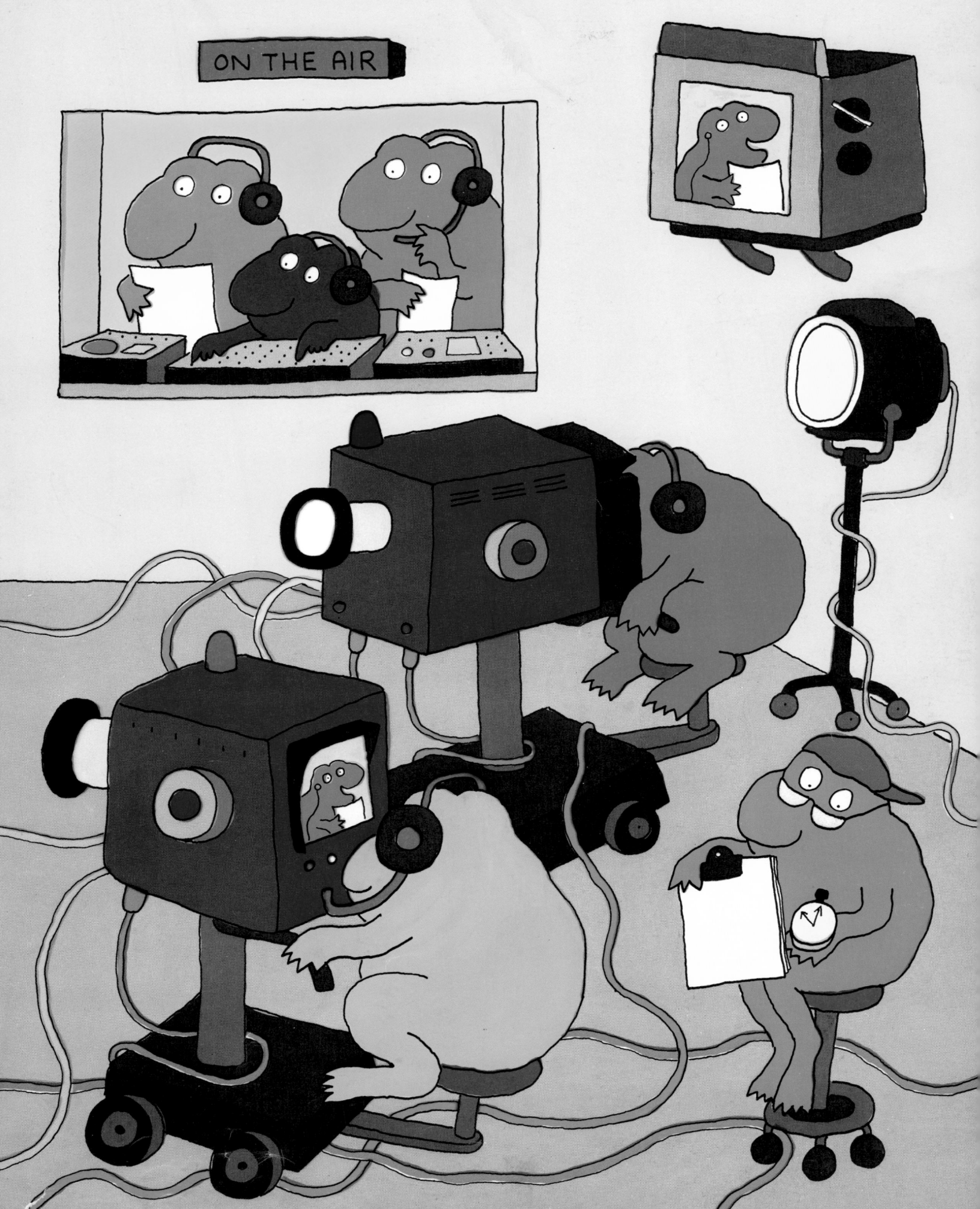

He blurt, blurt, blurts the news to the whole wide world!

The End